THE
COMPACT
CLARINET

*A complete guide
to the clarinet and
ten great composers*

written by
Barrie Carson Turner

MACMILLAN

First published 1996 by Macmillan Children's Books
a division of Macmillan Publishers Limited
25 Eccleston Place, London SW1W 9NF
and Basingstoke

Associated companies throughout the world

ISBN 0 333 64032 2

A CIP catalogue record for this book is available from the British Library.

Typeset by Macmillan Children's Books
Colour repro by Track QSP Ltd
Printed in Singapore

Text written by Barrie Carson Turner

Designer: Nigel Davies
Commissioning Editor: Susie Gibbs
Art Director: Anne Glenn
CD Consultant: Tony Locantro
Picture Researcher: Josine Meijer
Project Editor: Jane Robertson

Contents

OVERTURE

Playing and listening to music, as well as learning about it, is one of the most popular and exciting pastimes in the world today.

The clarinet is one of the most played of all woodwind instruments, and it can be heard in almost every kind of music – orchestral, wind band, chamber music, jazz or pop. Its musical reputation is well deserved. It has a clear and expressive sound which is ideal for solo work, whether playing in an orchestra or a small ensemble. The clarinet is particularly suitable for children to learn, as unlike many other instruments, 'real tunes' can be played in a very short time.

We are not sure exactly who made the first clarinet, but it was probably a German instrument maker, Johann Christoph Denner, living in Nuremberg in about 1700. The clarinet was developed from an older folk instrument, the *chalumeau*. A great variety of folk clarinets are still played today in various parts of the world. In India the *pungi* is made from two parallel canes glued together, while a large gourd surrounds and protects the reeds. This is the traditional snake-charmer's pipe.

The clarinet was at one time made from boxwood or rosewood, but today it is made from a very heavy wood called African blackwood. A good quality plastic clarinet is also available, although it may be some years before it is taken up by professional players. On pages 18 and 19 you will see photographs of a modern clarinet maker's workshop. Many of the tools you see in the pictures have not changed in design for over two hundred years.

The audio compact disc from EMI features extracts of music written by each of the ten composers in the book. The short section *ON THE CD*, which appears in the text for each composer, tells you a little about the music.

Whether you are already a clarinettist, just beginning lessons or simply interested in clarinet playing, *The Compact Clarinet* will add to the range of your knowledge and understanding of the clarinet.

THE CLARINET FAMILY

Sopranino

The sopranino clarinet is a popular member of the military band, where its high shrill tone adds sharpness to the mellow sound of the other woodwind and brass instruments. It is seldom seen in orchestras, although composers occasionally call for its bright and breezy sound, often giving it a descriptive role to play.

Above: The word 'sopranino' means 'a little soprano' – that is, a very high instrument. The sopranino clarinet is the highest clarinet in general use today. It measures about 49cm long, three quarters of the length of the orchestral clarinet.

Above: The clarinet's full name is 'soprano clarinet'. The name 'clarinet' derives from the Italian word clarinetto *which means 'little trumpet'. The name was chosen to describe the clarinet's powerful but gentle sound. The instrument measures 66cm long.*

Clarinet

The clarinet's reedy sound is produced by a thin piece of cane that vibrates to the force of the player's breath. The clarinettist has a selection of reeds of various strengths to choose from, depending on whether they want the sound of their instrument to be strident or more gentle. The clarinet blends well with almost all other instruments, especially flute, bassoon, horn and strings.

Alto clarinet

The alto clarinet was invented in 1810 by the German clarinettist and instrument maker Iwan Müller. It is lower in pitch, and much longer and larger than the soprano clarinet. To allow the instrument to be held easily, the mouthpiece is situated in an extra piece of tubing called a 'crook', which is bent back towards the player. To avoid directing the sound of the instrument towards the floor, the flared 'bell' is curved up and points towards the listener.

Basset-horn

The basset-horn is perfectly described by its name – 'basset' means 'little bass' (referring to its deep notes). Today the basset-horn looks similar to the alto clarinet, although a little larger. The basset-horn was a favourite instrument of Mozart, who included it in his *Requiem*. Mendelssohn also wrote for the basset-horn, and Richard Strauss scored for it in several of his operas. Today basset-horn parts are sometimes played by the alto clarinet.

Left: *The basset-horn's original curved construction was replaced in the early nineteenth century by a straight design which has remained the usual shape of the instrument ever since.*

Bass clarinet

The bass clarinet, larger again than the alto clarinet and basset-horn, is the lowest member of the clarinet family in general use. The earliest bass clarinets date from the end of the eighteenth century, and were probably intended as wind band instruments. During the course of the nineteenth century, however, the bass clarinet slowly began to appear in orchestral scores. The French composer Giacomo Meyerbeer led the way in 1836 by writing an important part for it in his opera *Les Huguenots*.

Left: *Because the bass clarinet is of considerable weight, it is held either in a sling around the player's neck or supported by a metal spike.*

Contrabass clarinet

The contrabass clarinet is the most recently invented instrument of the clarinet family, and dates from the late nineteenth century. It is a curiously shaped instrument, looking nothing at all like a clarinet. 'Contra' means 'lower octave': to produce such low notes the tube of the clarinet needs to be very long.

Left: *Early versions of the contrabass clarinet looked like a larger version of the bass clarinet. However recent instruments are made entirely of metal, with the tube curled around itself and the bell at the top.*

WIND INSTRUMENTS AROUND THE WORLD

Alboka *(Spain)*
The alboka, from Northern Spain, originated in the Middle East. Like the Welsh pibcorn it belongs to the 'hornpipe' family, and has long been associated with shepherds. It is played with the blowing horn pressed tightly against the mouth, and has a distinct nasal sound.

Pibcorn *(Wales)*
The Welsh pibcorn has a horn at both ends. The name is made up of 'pib' meaning pipe, and 'corn', an old word for horn. The reed is hidden inside the horn at the blowing end of the instrument. Players do not take the reed between their lips, but blow the instrument by pressing it tightly against their mouth.

Zummara *(Egypt)*
The Egyptian zummara is a double clarinet, made up of two pipes which are sounded simultaneously. Players use 'circular breathing' to play the instrument – breathing in through their nose, and out through their mouth at the same time. This clever technique means an uninterrupted flow of sound can be produced.

Diple *(Dalmatia)*
As a clarinet the Dalmatian diple varies considerably in design from region to region, and can also take the form of a bagpipe. Its reedy, strident tone makes it very much suited to outdoor playing. For this reason it is often used by shepherds for signalling, and at village celebrations.

Xiao *(China)*
Xiao (pronounced *hiss-ow*) means 'little flute'. The instrument is one of China's most ancient wind instruments, and dates back 3000 years. It was at one time played by shepherds, but now it is more likely to be bought as a toy. The xiao in the picture is a child's instrument which was bought in Shanghai in 1902.

Pungi *(India)*
The Indian pungi is made of two parallel canes glued together. A large dried gourd surrounds the reeds, the player blowing into the neck of the gourd. The left pipe of the instrument plays a drone only (one note sounding all the time throughout the piece) while the right pipe plays the melody. The pungi is the traditional snake-charmer's pipe.

INSTRUMENTAL GROUPS

Duets

A 'duet' is a piece for two performers. In the picture below the clarinet plays a duet with the bagpipes. Duets were popular in the eighteenth century but in the last two centuries duet writing seems to have been neglected.

Clarinet and piano

Woodwind instruments like the clarinet blend well with the piano, and composers have written a variety of imaginative works for this combination of instruments, often writing for specific performers. Sonatas tend to be the most serious works; other music is in a much lighter vein, such as the 'Rhapsody for clarinet and piano' by Debussy.

Music for solo clarinet

Composers seldom write for solo unaccompanied 'melody' instruments (instruments that can only play one line of music at once – like the clarinet). This is probably because two players are easier to listen to than one, but also an accompaniment allows a soloist to take an occasional rest. Writing for an unaccompanied solo instrument is very difficult, but some twentieth-century composers such as Stravinsky have written successfully for solo clarinet.

Trios

A trio is a piece for three instruments, although 'clarinet trio' does not usually mean a piece for three clarinets, but rather a trio in which a single clarinet is given a prominent part. Mozart wrote the first clarinet trio, still heard in concerts today, for clarinet, piano and viola.

Quartets and quintets

Although early composers for the clarinet, such as Carl Stamitz, wrote quartets and quintets for the instrument, these works are seldom heard today. It is Mozart again, with his quintet for piano, oboe, clarinet, horn and bassoon, who alone represents early clarinet chamber music. Quintets were later composed by Beethoven and Brahms and a few twentieth-century composers. In 1941 the French composer Olivier Messiaen wrote his *Quartet for the end of time* for clarinet, violin, cello and piano while in a prisoner-of-war camp.

Clarinet concertos

The word 'concerto' was originally used to describe a performance 'together'. Over the last 250 years, however, it has come to mean a composition usually for one solo instrument and orchestra. Clarinet concertos have been written throughout this period, although the only eighteenth-century concerto regularly heard today is by Mozart. In the twentieth century there have been several exciting new concertos for clarinet, including Stravinsky's *Ebony Concerto*, a jazz-style work written for the American clarinettist Benny Goodman.

The clarinet in jazz

The clarinet was for many years a leading instrument in jazz, popularized by such solo performers as Sidney Bechet, Benny Goodman and Woody Herman. Jazz musicians were impressed with the smooth sounds readily available from the instrument, its wide dynamic range and robust tone. Today the clarinet is no longer a leading member of the jazz scene, although it remains an essential member of the Dixieland band.

THE HISTORY OF THE CLARINET

Nuremberg in 1725, where the first clarinet was made.

Johann Christoph Denner

Music historians believe that the first clarinet was made in 1700 by Johann Christoph Denner, a German instrument maker living in Nuremberg. The first ever mention of the clarinet is in an order dated 1710 for twenty-three woodwind instruments, including clarinets, made by Jacob Denner, Johann's son. The clarinet was modelled on an earlier instrument called the *chalumeau*.

The chalumeau

The chalumeau was at its best playing low notes, whereas the high notes were of poor quality. Denner discovered that by adding an additional finger hole in the upper end of the tube, a higher range of notes could be obtained. To improve the reliability of the high notes, the thick, crudely shaped reed of the chalumeau was made narrower and more slender. The first clarinet was in fact simply a high-sounding chalumeau.

Early clarinets were shriller, and more penetrating than the instruments we know today. They sounded more like a trumpet when heard from a distance.

Johann Christoph Denner died in 1707, but his work was carried on by his son, who reshaped the end of the tube into a 'bell' (which looked like a small trumpet bell) to improve the projection of sound, and increased the range of notes.

To improve the accuracy of drilling the tube, and to make tuning easier, the body of the new instrument was made in several closely fitting jointed sections. The pitch of the instrument is related to the overall length of the tube, and the makers came up with the ingenious idea of duplicating one of the clarinet joints in a variety of lengths – these were known by their French name, *corps de rechange*.

Above: The chalumeau, predecessor of the clarinet, showing the characteristically wide reed. The instrument sounds like a low clarinet.

Below: High-pitched clarinets:
a) sopranino
b) soprano in B flat
c) soprano in A.

A clarinet player from *The Clarinet* Instructor *published in 1780.*

The English clarinettist T. L. Willman, an illustration from his clarinet tutor (c.1825).

Early instruments had the reed facing up, and bound to the mouthpiece with twine. Later on instrument makers had repositioned the reed to rest on the lower lip.

During the eighteenth century, instrument makers continued to remodel and improve the clarinet, concentrating particularly on the fingering system. By 1750 the clarinet had made great strides since Denner's first model, and composers were beginning to include it in their works. The clarinet was more acceptable as an orchestral instrument now that it could tune to any orchestral pitch. Orchestras in Paris and the famed Mannheim orchestra already employed regular clarinettists. Military bands too were interested in the clarinet, with its relatively easy playing technique, increasingly using it in preference to the oboe. In 1764 the first clarinet tutor, by the German virtuoso Valentin Roeser, was published.

By the end of the eighteenth century, to accommodate the demand for precision tuning, clarinet makers built clarinets in different keys. Because of the construction of the clarinet and its fingering system, it was easy playing in some keys and more difficult in others.

Iwan Müller

In 1809 the young German clarinettist Iwan Müller produced a clarinet with a new mechanical action, and finger holes placed more accurately than ever before. The result was an instrument of improved intonation (tuning), which understandably became very popular. In 1822 Müller published a clarinet tutor which featured the new instrument and was granted permission to dedicate the tutor to King George IV. Müller's clarinet remained popular until the beginning of the twentieth century.

Theobald Boehm

In 1832 the instrument maker Theobald Boehm was working on improving the flute mechanism. When his work was complete the French clarinettist Hyacinthe Klosé and the Paris instrument maker Louis-Auguste Buffet adapted the Boehm flute mechanism to the clarinet. The idea was successful, although players were generally reluctant at first to take up an instrument which would mean learning an entirely new fingering system.

As the century wore on, other makers, including the instrument maker Adolphe Sax, continued to adjust and modify the clarinet. Today a variety of different instruments and fingering systems are in use, although the Boehm system remains the most popular.

Above: George IV of England by Gainsborough, 1781.

a)   b)   c)   d)

Left: Low-pitched clarinets:
a) alto
b) basset-horn
c) bass
d) contrabass.

HOW THE CLARINET WORKS

Wind instruments produce their sound from a vibrating column of air inside a hollow body. In the case of the clarinet the air is set in motion by a reed, activated by the player's breath. The instrument modifies and amplifies the vibrations from the reed, turning them into sound.

The length of a tube (the body of the instrument) controls the pitch – how high or low the note is. A long tube will produce low notes, and a short tube high notes. By opening the finger holes in preset patterns a scale of notes can be obtained. By pressing the 'speaker key' the clarinettist is able to play notes higher up the instrument.

The **keywork** on the clarinet looks very complicated, but in fact is designed to make the clarinet much easier to play. Many keys cover holes which the fingers cannot reach.

The shape of the **bell** helps to project the sound outwards from the instrument.

Fingers press the **keys** to open and close the holes. Some keys are coupled to others and are activated automatically when another key is pressed. The clarinet has seventeen keys.

Lower (or right-hand) joint

The modern clarinet is made in five sections or **joints**. The **'tenon-and-socket' joints** fit together very tightly to ensure there is no leakage of air, which would affect the tone of the instrument.

The top teeth rest on the top of the wedge-shaped **mouthpiece**. The reed (which is underneath) rests on the lower lip which is slightly curved over the teeth.

The **barrel** is used for 'fine tuning' the instrument when necessary. By pulling the barrel out slightly, away from the top joint, the tube of the clarinet is made longer, and therefore the instrument will sound slightly lower. Some players use two barrels of different lengths to maintain tuning.

The **ligature** holds the reed tightly in place.

The **reed** fits over a slot in the mouthpiece which forms the end of the tube. The edges of the reed are secured by the ligature, but the main area of the reed is left free to vibrate.

Upper (or left-hand) joint

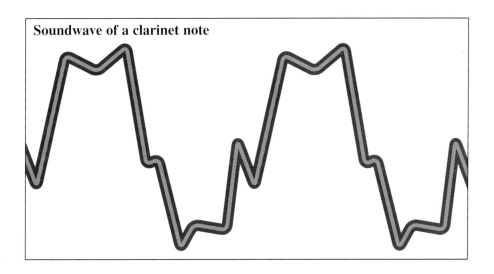

The **mouthpiece cap** protects the reed when the instrument is being carried, or is not in use.

Soundwave of a clarinet note

HOW THE CLARINET IS MADE

The **barrel** serves little or no real acoustic purpose, but remains as a decorative feature and an occasional tuning device. The wood is first crudely shaped and drilled, and then worked and bored to its final shape, and decorated.

The elegant **bell** begins life as a pyramid-shaped block of wood. To achieve the exact trumpet shape requires considerable woodworking proficiency.

The tube of the **upper joint** is first shaped to leave three wide bands of wood running close together at one end. Each band is then carefully pared to leave three raised **finger rests**, which ensure the finger holes, when covered, remain airtight.

The clarinet was at one time made from boxwood or rosewood, but today the modern clarinet is made from the heavy 'African blackwood'. For almost fifty years instrument makers have experimented with suitable plastics to find a replacement for wood that sounds just as good. Today a good-quality plastic clarinet is available, although it may be some years before it is taken up by professional players.

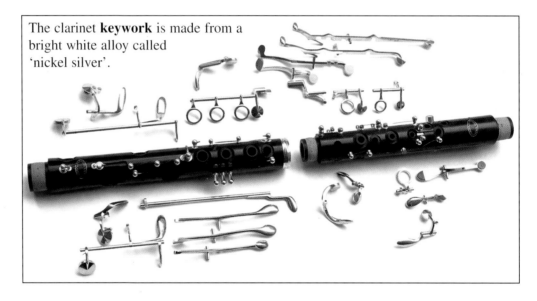

The clarinet **keywork** is made from a bright white alloy called 'nickel silver'.

The **tenon-and-socket joints** use a band of cork to help maintain airtightness and a close fit. Here the cork for one of the joints is being smoothed and trimmed on the workshop lathe.

Fine adjustments are made to one of the **keys.**
The keywork of the clarinet must be reliable
and responsive to a player's touch.

The workshop displays a wealth of tools.

The clarinet maker uses a **reemer** to enlarge
one of the holes, to modify the pitch.

Using a very thin piece of
paper, the pads are tested
to ensure they are pressing
correctly on the holes.

HOW THE CLARINET IS PLAYED

Breathing

Clarinettists breathe through the mouth when they play. How a clarinettist breathes is one of the most important parts of playing the instrument, because it affects every detail of performance. Both the taking in of breath and its controlled release are equally important.

Tonguing

Clarinet players 'tongue' a note by first placing the tip of their tongue lightly against the reed, and then pulling it back to release the breath and so sound the note. Tonguing is used to ensure that notes begin with precision and crispness.

Phrasing

Phrasing is common to nearly all instruments. A 'phrase' is like a musical sentence, and gives music shape and expression. Clarinet players phrase notes by joining them together smoothly in one breath.

Louds and softs

The clarinet has the greatest powers of *crescendo* (getting louder) and *diminuendo* (getting softer) of all the woodwind instruments. The clarinet is also much admired for its *pianissimo* (very quiet) playing.

The clarinet is one of the most popular of all woodwind instruments, and it can be heard in almost every kind of music, whether orchestral, wind band, chamber music, jazz or pop. It has a clear and expressive sound which is ideal for solo work. The lowest notes which have a reedy hollow sound are unlike those of any other instrument. The clarinet is particularly suitable for young children to learn, as unlike many other instruments 'real' tunes can be played in a very short time.

Fingering
The right thumb fits snugly under the thumbhook on the underside of the lower joint, and carries the weight of the clarinet.

Staccato
The Italian word *staccato* means 'detached'. In clarinet playing, staccato notes are all tongued separately. The use of a certain amount of staccato adds elegance to clarinet playing.

Tremolo
This Italian word means 'trembling'. To clarinet players, *tremolo* means playing two alternate notes in rapid succession. Played low down, a tremolo can sound mysterious and almost sinister, while played high up, it is shrill and exciting.

Vibrato
Vibrato, another Italian word, means 'shaking'. If you listen very carefully to a clarinettist using vibrato you will hear a slight wavering (rising and falling) of pitch.

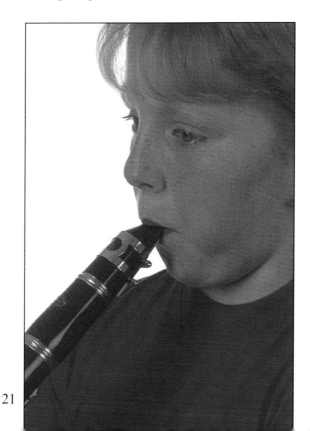

Arpeggios, leaps and scales
The clarinet is a very agile instrument. Leaping from one note to another, even with large gaps in between, is no problem for this accommodating instrument. Composers have occasionally used clarinet leaps for comic effects. Playing scales and arpeggios is also very easy on the clarinet.

Glissando
'Glissando' is actually the French word *glisser*, meaning 'to slide', deliberately made to sound Italian! A glissando is a 'slide' (like a fast scale) over several notes. One of the most famous glissandos ever written is for clarinet – the beginning of Gershwin's *Rhapsody in Blue*.

Multiphonics
It is possible with care to play more than one note at a time on the clarinet (and on other wind instruments also). Such 'chords' of notes are called *multiphonics* ('multiple sounds'), producing a strange and almost eerie sound. To achieve them involves complex fingering.

MOZART
1756–1791

Wolfgang Amadeus Mozart met the Austrian clarinettist Anton Stadler and became good friends with him (like Mozart he was a Freemason). Mozart also wrote important clarinet parts in his operas for Stadler, as well as several chamber works, and of course composed the much-loved Clarinet Concerto.

Right: *Frontispiece from Mozart's opera* La clemenza di Tito (*'The clemency of Tito'*) *which included a virtuoso clarinet part especially written for Anton Stadler.*

Mozart showed his musical gifts at a very early age, taking formal keyboard and theory lessons with his father, Leopold, and by the age of four we are told he could play his lessons 'perfectly'. When he composed his first pieces he was unable to write the music down, and so his father wrote it down for him.

While Mozart was copying out a symphony by the German composer Carl Friedrich Abel, he first encountered the clarinet. At the time, in 1764, the Mozarts were living in London, and it is possible that Mozart first heard the clarinet at a London concert.

Mozart wrote his first work for the clarinet in 1771, a Divertimento (a light piece written for entertainment purposes). Six years later he visited Mannheim and was impressed by the clarinet playing in the famous orchestra at the Electoral palace. Writing to his father he said, 'Alas, if only we also had clarinets'.

The first work Mozart wrote for Anton Stadler was a trio, scored for the unusual combination of clarinet, viola and piano. Mozart wrote this beautiful work in 1786 at a time when he was virtually penniless. The trio is occasionally known by its strange name of the Kegelstatt ('Skittle Alley') trio, because it is said the work was composed at a skittle game!

Heute Sonntags, den 28. Februar 1796.
wird
durch die besondere Gnade Sr. Majestät des Königs
die Wittwe des verstorbenen Kapellmeisters Mozart
auf dem Königlichen Opern-Theater,
unterstützt von den Königlichen Sängern und Sängerinnen, und der Königlichen Kapelle, die Ehre haben aufzuführen,
das letzte Werk ihres verstorbenen Mannes:

LA CLEMENZA DI TITO.

Erster Theil.
Ouverture aus der Zauberflöte.
Arie, gesungen von Madame Righini, komponirt von Mozart.
Fagott-Conzert, gesetzt und geblasen von Herrn Ritter.
Arie, gesungen von Demoiselle Schmalz, komponirt von Mozart.

Zweyter Theil.
Der Auszug der wesentlichsten Stücke, aus der Oper:
La Clemenza di Tito, von Mozart; worinn Madame Schick, Madame Righini, Demoiselle Schmalz, Herr Fischer, Herr Hurka, und Madame Mozart singen werden.

Die Texte zur Musik werden beym Eingange für 4 Groschen ausgegeben.

Preise der Plätze.
Die Person zahlet im Ersten Range	1 Rthlr.	8 Gr.
Im zweyten Range	1 Rthlr.	
In den Parterre-Logen		16 Gr.
Im dritten Range		16 Gr.
Parterre		12 Gr.

Billets auf ganze Logen im Ersten Range, sind bey der Wittwe Mozart, in der Neuen Friedrichsstraße, ip Schielens Haufe, neben der Garnison-Kirche, die übrigen Logen und einzelnen Plätze, von Morgens um 9, bis Mittags um 1 Uhr bey dem Kastellan des Opernhauses, zu haben.

Der Anfang ist um halb Sechs Uhr.

Left: Mozartplatz, in Salzburg, where Mozart was composer to the Archbishop.

Below: An informal street performance. Outdoor 'serenades' were commonplace in the Vienna of Mozart's day.

Mozart only gradually began to use clarinets in his orchestral works, including them in just two of his symphonies, although he later added them to two others. His last work for clarinet – the Clarinet Concerto – is his most famous, and one of the most well-known works ever written for the instrument.

ON THE CD
Clarinet Quintet in A, K581
I. Allegro

Mozart wrote the Clarinet Quintet, for clarinet and strings, in 1789, and Anton Stadler gave the work its first performance in Vienna the same year. In the opening of the first movement the clarinet plays a beautiful decorative accompaniment figure, assuming more important thematic material later in the movement.

Left: The palace at Mannheim where the Elector Carl Theodor brought together the finest composers and musicians to serve in his household. By the time of Mozart's visit the orchestra could boast two good clarinettists.

BEETHOVEN
1770–1827

Ludwig van Beethoven was the first major composer to score for the clarinet in all his mature orchestral compositions.

Beethoven received his first music lessons from his father. At eleven, he began studies with the court organist Christian Gottlob Neefe, who arranged for the boy to have one of his earliest compositions published.

Beethoven was born into the age of the clarinet. For almost a hundred years the clarinet had hovered on the sidelines of music. But with Beethoven's support its acceptance into the orchestra was finally assured. The wind octet (a piece for eight instruments), written for oboes, clarinets, bassoons and horns was composed when the composer was only twenty-two. In the same year Beethoven wrote three Duos (duets) for clarinet and bassoon.

Most of Beethoven's compositions for wind were written on commission; and commissions (paid requests for compositions) made up a valuable source of a composer's income.

Throughout his life Beethoven moved easily among the nobility and the rich. The wind quintet written in 1796, for instance, is dedicated to Prince von Schwarzenberg. A dedication by Beethoven almost always indicated a paid commission.

Above: Christian Gottlob Neefe (1748–98) said of Beethoven, 'this young genius will surely become a second Amadeus Mozart if he continues as he has begun'.

Right: A room in the house where Beethoven was born. The building is now a Beethoven museum.

Bonn, where Beethoven was born in 1770. His father Johann was determined that young Ludwig should become a child prodigy, like Mozart.

After the turn of the century Beethoven wrote virtually no more wind music. This may have been because the popular serenades and divertimentos of Haydn's and Mozart's day were no longer in fashion. Another explanation may have been, as Beethoven said in a letter to his publishers, that he had simply 'moved on' to bigger and better things. Of course Beethoven did not abandon the clarinet completely – it still had an extremely important role to play in his orchestral music.

Beethoven performed in public concert halls such as the Theater an der Wien (above) as well as in the houses of the Viennese nobility, often playing his own compositions.

Right: *Beethoven's house in Bonngasse, Bonn. The composer was born in the attic on the right-hand side of the picture.*

ON THE CD
Clarinet Trio in B flat Op.11
I. Allegro con brio

Beethoven wrote his trio for clarinet, piano and cello in 1797, on a commission from the Countess von Thun. On the score Beethoven indicates that the clarinet part can also be played by the violin.

CRUSELL
1775–1838

Bernhard Henrik Crusell was born in Finland to a family of bookbinders and became one of Finland's most highly regarded composers. He first heard the clarinet at the age of four and began formal clarinet lessons at the age of eight. Within a short time he had impressed his teacher and family with his astounding progress.

Stockholm in Crusell's day. Crusell's informative autobiography tells us much about life in this thriving city.

Crusell's music career began at the early age of twelve when he joined a military band in the Finnish town of Sveaborg as a clarinettist. In 1791 he moved with the band to Stockholm, where he continued to concentrate on improving his playing technique. In 1793 he had his first major performing break when he was appointed principal clarinettist in the Duke Regent's band in Stockholm.

By 1798 Crusell had moved to Berlin where he began clarinet lessons with the noted teacher Franz Tausch. And in 1803 he studied with the French player Jean Xavier Lefèvre in Paris. Gradually Crusell was making a name for himself as a distinguished soloist, but his interest in composition was growing too, and he took lessons with several eminent composers, including François-Joseph Gossec, a popular Parisian musical figure of the day.

Composers have often used folk tunes in their compositions. The song Crusell uses in his Variations for Clarinet *may well have been sung in scenes such as this.*

Left: *Mikhail Ivanovich Glinka (1804–57), one of the first major Russian composers, greatly admired Crusell's music. Speaking of one of Crusell's clarinet quartets, he said 'this music produced an unbelievable effect on me'.*

Alexander I, Tsar of Russia from 1801–25.

ON THE CD
Clarinet Concerto No. 2
in F minor Op. 5
III. Rondo: Allegretto

Through his association with the Swedish court Crusell came into contact with royalty and the nobility of his day. The Clarinet Concerto No. 2, one of the finest of Crusell's compositions for the instrument, is dedicated to Alexander I, Tsar of Russia.

Crusell's important works are the three clarinet concertos, written in 1811, 1816 and 1829. His Clarinet Concerto No. 1 is dedicated to a Swedish count, a close friend who often invited Crusell to his home, while the third concerto is dedicated to the Crown Prince of Sweden and Norway, whose band Crusell directed and conducted each summer.

Crusell also wrote a 'triple concerto' (which he called a 'sinfonia concertante') for clarinet, horn and bassoon. Another work, a set of variations for clarinet and orchestra, uses a Swedish drinking song as its theme. As a composer Crusell was admired particularly for his melodic invention.

Throughout his life Crusell held important playing and directing posts, including that of music director for the chapel of the Swedish court, as well as for the royal regiment. Towards the end of his life he wrote an autobiography, which offers music historians many fascinating details about his life and times.

SPOHR
1784–1859

Spohr was only ten years old when he made his first attempts at composition. Both his parents were musical, and they sent their son to Brunswick to study music where, at fifteen, after appearing in a successful concert of his own works, he was employed by the Duke as one of his chamber musicians.

Although Spohr began his adult professional life as a violinist, his developing musicianship soon led him more in the direction of composition. He idolized Mozart, and it was perhaps Mozart's great clarinet concerto that inspired him to start composing himself: between 1810 and 1828 he wrote four works for the clarinet.

The highly respected German clarinettist Simon Hermstedt, to whom Spohr dedicated his first concerto, gave the première of all four concertos. The clarinet as a solo instrument was still relatively new in Spohr's day, although

As a composer Louis Spohr was highly regarded – he was made an honorary member of thirty-eight music societies in Germany and abroad.

The town of Brunswick where Spohr was born. Although the family moved elsewhere in 1796, Spohr's parents sent him back to study here.

La Scala, still one of the greatest opera houses in the world, was the scene of one of the Spohrs' most successful concerts in 1816.

it was well established in the orchestra. Spohr was clearly fond of the new instrument, giving it an important solo part in one of his songs.

In 1806 Spohr married Dorette Scheidler, a harpist, and they made many successful tours together, while Spohr continued to compose prolifically. During this period he wrote two of his most respected chamber works for clarinet: the Nonet (for nine instruments) was written in 1813, and the Octet (for eight instruments) followed the next year. Spohr also used the clarinet in his Septet (seven instruments) of 1853 and the Quintet of 1820.

Spohr also wrote several virtuoso solo works for clarinet. 'Display' works for individual instruments were always popular on concert programmes, and much enjoyed by audiences. In Spohr's clarinet variations of 1809 he used a theme from his own opera *Alruna*. Despite his popularity during his lifetime, after his death almost all Spohr's works fell into obscurity.

Dorette Scheidler, Spohr's wife who, as well as being a harpist, was a competent pianist and violinist. Spohr was only twenty when he married.

The music room in Spohr's house, with the composer's grand piano in the corner.

ON THE CD
Octet in E, Op.32
Adagio – Allegro

Spohr wrote his Octet in 1814. The instruments the composer uses – mixed woodwind, brass and strings – are unusual as a chamber group. The clarinet, two horns, violin, two violas, cello and double bass, however, blend perfectly together.

29

WEBER

1786–1826

Carl Maria von Weber was related to Mozart by marriage, and like Mozart, he died young. Weber's chamber works include several compositions for clarinet, although he was really more interested in composing operas and large orchestral works than small chamber compositions.

Weber's father was music director of his own travelling theatrical group, the Weber Theatre Company. While touring southern Germany young Carl took his first music lessons at the age of three with his stepbrother Fridolin, who said the boy would never become a musician! But by the age of eleven Weber was studying with Michael Haydn – younger brother of the great Joseph Haydn. By the time he was fifteen he was determined that composition would be his life.

Over the next few years Weber took on a curious mixture of posts including the conductorship of the opera at Breslau. He was also secretary to the brother of the King of Württemberg. Somehow, through the foolishness of his father he found himself being charged with embezzlement and expelled from the country! Forced to seek residence elsewhere, Weber settled in Darmstadt where he met the greatest German clarinettist, Heinrich Joseph Baermann. Their friendship was to prove extremely fruitful.

In 1811, Weber and Baermann gave a successful joint concert in Munich which

Salzburg cathedral where Weber was a chorister. In 1806 he accidentally drank a glass of nitric acid thinking it was wine. This destroyed the composer's singing voice as well as seriously affecting his speech.

Ludwigstrasse in Munich at the time of Weber's meeting with the clarinettist Heinrich Joseph Baermann. Baermann was principal clarinettist of the Munich court orchestra.

Wolf's Glen scene from Weber's opera Der Freishütz. *In highly romantic works, like this tale based on German folk lore, Weber was at his best as a dramatic orchestrator.*

included Weber's new Clarinet Concertino (a small concerto) written especially for Baermann. King Maximilian I, present in the audience, immediately commissioned two full-scale clarinet concertos from Weber. After further travelling and performing, Weber returned to Munich to set off again with Baermann on a joint concert tour.

It is likely that Weber's friendship with Baermann prompted most of his compositions for clarinet, although Weber also met the clarinettist, Simon Hermstedt, and was invited to compose for him. Weber also wrote several small chamber works for the clarinet, including a set of variations on a theme from his opera *Silvana,* and a clarinet quintet.

ON THE CD
Grand Duo Concertant,
Op. 48 III. Rondo: Allegro

Weber wrote three works for clarinet and piano. The finest and most well known is the *Grand duo Concertant.* The title 'grand' tells us the composer considered this an important work and *duo* ('duet') tells us that both clarinet and piano are of equal musical importance.

ROSSINI
1792–1868

It is likely that Gioachino Rossini was first introduced to the clarinet through his father, whose early musical career had involved him in military band work, an area of music in which the clarinet was well established.

A t an early age Rossini's father taught him the French horn and by the time he was twelve Gioachino was composing his first pieces.

When the family moved to Bologna in 1804, Rossini entered the music school, where he studied other orchestral instruments and began to make his first efforts at orchestration. During this period he wrote several student works, and won a prize for a cantata.

Left: Napoleon at the Bridge of Arcole *by Gros. The Napoleonic Wars caused tremendous political upheaval throughout Europe. The Rossini family was drawn into this, especially Rossini's father who spent a short time in prison in 1800.*

Right: Scene from The Barber of Seville, *considered one of Rossini's greatest operas. At its first performance rival supporters of a similar opera based on the same play nearly caused a riot in the theatre.*

In his orchestrations Rossini especially favoured the clarinet and the woodwind family: we find many fine clarinet solos in his opera scores. One of Rossini's most famous clarinet tunes is in the overture to his comic opera *The Barber of Seville*, written in 1816.

But there are other equally fine ones in *The Thieving Magpie*, and in another popular opera, *La Cenerentola* ('Cinderella').

Rossini also wrote several works specifically for the clarinet. In 1809 while still a student, he wrote a set of variations for clarinet, string quartet and orchestra – *Variazioni a più istrumenti obbligati*. Three years later he wrote a similar piece – *Andante e Tema con variazioni* ('Andante and theme with variations'), this time for four solo wind instruments – flute, clarinet, horn and bassoon.

Rossini also wrote several military band pieces, including three marches written in 1837, commissioned for the marriage of the Duc d'Orléans. And in the last year of his life he wrote a band piece entitled *La corona d'Italia* ('The Crown of Italy'), probably composed for an official function.

Right: Bologna in the nineteenth century. The Rossini family moved to Bologna in 1804 where Gioachino began his first formal music studies.

Rossini's funeral in Paris was attended by thousands of mourners. In his will the composer left a large endowment for the establishment of a music school at his birthplace, Pesaro.

ON THE CD
Introduction, Theme and Variations for clarinet and orchestra

Rossini wrote this piece – another work in the popular variation style – in 1809, when he was a student at Bologna's Liceo Musicale.

MENDELSSOHN
1809–1847

Felix Mendelssohn did not write much for solo clarinet, but the instrument was very important to him in his orchestral music. Particularly loved among Mendelssohn's orchestral works is the Italian Symphony; the clarinets and other wind instruments are responsible for the lively accompaniment figure of the opening.

Mendelssohn was born into an artistic and well-to-do German banking family. This enabled him to have the finest musicians as teachers, who encouraged in every way to pursue his musical talents.

At fifteen Mendelssohn wrote his first piece for clarinet – a sonata with piano accompaniment – for his friend, the sixteen-year-old Carl Baermann. The same year, while on holiday, Mendelssohn wrote for clarinet again – an overture for wind band.

Left: Carl Friedrich Zelter (1758–1832), teacher and composer and a leading figure in Berlin's musical life, taught Mendelssohn theory and composition.

Above: Berlin, Unter den Linden. In 1811 the Mendelssohn family moved to Berlin where Felix spent his childhood.

Left and below: *On a trip to Scotland in 1829 Mendelssohn visited the Hebrides, and in particular Fingal's Cave, the huge sea cavern on the Isle of Staffa. The cave and its surrounds created a great impression on Mendelssohn, and inspired several musical thoughts which he jotted down on the spot, and later used in his 'Hebrides Overture'.*

Mendelssohn composed several other overtures during his mature years. Some of this music includes descriptions of the sea; the smooth, flowing sound of the clarinet associates well with such images. In the exciting 'Hebrides' overture the clarinet introduces the beautiful second melody; and in the overture 'The Fair Melusina', written in 1833, the clarinet theme

Mendelssohn's house in Leipzig. The composer accepted the post of conductor of the famous Leipzig Gewandhaus orchestra in 1835.

represents the mermaid Melusina. The wind section of the orchestra also plays an important part in the overture 'Calm sea and prosperous voyage'.

In 1832 Mendelssohn wrote a Concert Piece for the unusual combination of clarinet, basset-horn and piano. This piece was nicknamed *The Battle of Prague*, as Mendelssohn had included in the score a theme by the Czech composer Koczwara who, forty-five years previously, had written a sonata of the same name. The Concert Piece was written for the brothers Heinrich and Carl Baermann.

ON THE CD
Concert Piece in D minor
for clarinet, basset-horn and
orchestra No.2 Op. 114
Presto – Andante – Allegretto grazioso

When Heinrich and Carl Baermann played through Mendelssohn's first Concert Piece, they were so taken with the music that they immediately commissioned a second similar work. Mendelssohn wrote the Concert Piece No. 2 in D minor in an amazingly short time, presenting the score to his friends in January 1833.

SCHUMANN
1810–1856

Robert Schumann's output was prolific, and included several chamber works for clarinet.

Below: *Zwickau, Saxony, where Schumann was born, the son of a bookseller. By the time he was eleven Schumann had written his first orchestral works.*

Robert Schumann showed his musical talents at an extremely early age, but his parents were determined that he should become a lawyer. However, he gave up his law studies to follow a musical career. Schumann wanted passionately to become a piano virtuoso, but a tragedy destroyed all hopes of a concert career. A sling-like device of his own invention, designed to strengthen the fourth finger of his right hand, resulted in a permanent disability. Fortunately he had a second musical interest – composition, and it was to this he now turned.

Above: *Friedrich Wieck (1785–1873), Schumann's piano teacher and Clara Schumann's father. It was while studying with Wieck that Schumann damaged his hand.*

Right: *Schumann with his wife Clara, who gave him much encouragement as a composer, and who was herself a fine pianist.*

Left: Spring *by Monet.
Schumann called his first
symphony the 'Spring' because
he watched the countryside
transform from winter into
spring outside his room as he
composed the music. The
clarinet plays an important
role throughout the work.*

Below: *The Dresden
Revolution, 1849, by Julius
Scholtz. The year of writing the
Phantasiestücke for clarinet was
no easy year for Schumann and
his wife Clara. Returning from
the country one day they found
Dresden in uproar, and only just
escaped in time to avoid
becoming involved in the
violence themselves.*

By Schumann's day the clarinet was a fully established member of the orchestra. The clarinet has the same smooth sound as the flute, and blends well with the other woodwind instruments. Composers were also beginning to appreciate the clarinet for its own beautiful sound, particularly appropriate in slow lyrical melodies.

In 1849, during a prolific spell of composing, Schumann wrote three pieces for clarinet and piano which he called *Phantasiestücke* ('Fantasy Pieces'). In another chamber work written the same year – the three Romances for oboe and piano – Schumann suggested the optional instruments of clarinet and violin.

Schumann was very much a romantic, in tune with his times, and this is reflected in his fanciful titles. In 1853, in the closing years of his composing

life, he wrote the *Märchenerzählungen* ('Fairytale pieces'). The four pieces are scored for piano, clarinet and viola, with the option of violin for the clarinet part. They comprise Schumann's last chamber music work.

ON THE CD
Phantasiestücke Op.73
III. Rasch und mit feuer –
Coda: Schneller

The 'Fantasy Pieces' for clarinet were always popular with Schumann's wife Clara, who used to play them with the famous clarinettist Richard Mühlfeld. The third piece in Schumann's *Phantasiestücke* is sprightly and quick, and Schumann marks it 'with fire'.

BRAHMS
1833–1897

Unfortunately for clarinet players and lovers of the instrument, Johannes Brahms only 'discovered' the clarinet towards the end of his life. But he left several pieces of fine chamber music as a worthy addition to the clarinettist's repertoire.

B rahms's father was a double bass player in Hamburg, and it was from him that Johannes received his first musical instruction. At the age of fourteen the young composer played in a public concert – his own set of piano variations, based on a folk song.

The clarinet first appears in Brahms's early orchestral works, featuring prominently in the two Serenades for small orchestra, written when the composer was in his middle twenties. The Serenades remind us of Mozart, as Brahms also preferred to write in classical forms. In the second Serenade the clarinets play a leading role right from the start: particularly beautiful is the clarinet and flute melody in the slow third movement.

Left: Freiburg, one of the towns where Brahms and Richard Mühlfeld performed the clarinet sonatas on their tour of Southern Germany in 1895.

Right: Chamber music playing was a popular pastime in the houses of the well-to-do. In this picture, the cello player has fallen asleep at the end of an evening's entertainment.

Meiningen, where through his good friend the Duke of Meiningen, Brahms met the clarinettist Richard Mühlfeld, for whom he wrote his clarinet pieces.

The Trio in A minor is the first of Brahms's chamber works to include clarinet. Brahms wrote all his clarinet works for the same performer, the German virtuoso Richard Mühlfeld, who he met at Meiningen. He was impressed not only by Mühlfeld's playing but also by the capabilities of the instrument itself. The Trio for clarinet, cello and piano, was written in the summer of 1891 in Brahms's favourite holiday resort of Bad Ischl.

When the work was finished, Brahms was so pleased with his efforts that he began a second piece – a quintet for clarinet and string quartet. In this work Brahms fully explores the expressive potential of the clarinet. At the opening of the first movement the instrument rises high above the violins – only to fall, later, to the rich, deep tones of its lowest register.

Brahms wrote all his solo clarinet pieces towards the end of his life, and perhaps for this reason these beautiful works have their own special poignancy.

Below: *This contemporary cartoon shows the composer on his way to The Red Hedgehog, a favourite inn. Brahms worked hard, but he also enjoyed a lively social life.*

ON THE CD
Clarinet Quintet
in B minor Op. 115
III. Andantino – Presto non
assai, ma con sentimento

The Clarinet Quintet was written in 1891, and is often considered the most beautiful of all of Brahms's chamber works. The piece is written for clarinet, two violins, viola, and cello.

REGER
1873–1916

When Max Reger was a young man Bach, Beethoven and Brahms were the composers he respected most, and his aim was to incorporate their style into his own works. His clarinet works especially show the influence of Brahms.

Below: J. S. Bach, one of Reger's earliest influences. Reger admired Bach's use of counterpoint (the setting of several strands of music one against the other) and used the technique in his own works.

Reger's father, Joseph Reger, was a keen amateur musician and played the oboe, clarinet and double bass. The Regers were determined that their son should take music lessons at the earliest opportunity, although it was not until he was approaching his teens that Reger began a formal music training. As a student under the local organist, he composed his first music, but also followed in his father's footsteps by training to be a teacher.

Reger had been introduced to the mellow sound of the clarinet through the playing of his father and music-making at home. He held Brahms in great respect as one of Germany's foremost composers, and in 1895 he sent one of his compositions to Brahms. The composer replied with encouraging remarks and a signed photograph!

In 1888, as a boy of fifteen, Reger travelled to hear Wagner's opera Parsifal *at Bayreuth. It was after seeing the opera that Reger decided to become a musician.*

Left: Reger had a quiet country upbringing in Bavaria in a household where music was always played and encouraged.

Within five years, and after Brahms's death, Reger wrote his own clarinet sonatas. They were performed two years later with Reger playing the piano and his friend Karl Wagner playing the clarinet.

In 1909, when Reger was Director of Music and Composition at Leipzig University, he wrote a third clarinet sonata. The influence of Brahms in this work is clear before a note is heard – Brahms's sonatas and clarinet trio have alternative string parts – Reger writes for 'clarinet or viola' on the score. Reger wrote his final piece for clarinet in 1916 – a quintet. He died suddenly a few months later after paying a visit to friends.

Right: In 1896 Reger was conscripted into military service which had a disruptive effect on his studies. As a student teacher he was only required to do a year's training, but he was released after only nine months because of ill health.

ON THE CD
Clarinet Quintet in A
Op. 146
II. – Vivace – un poco meno mosso
– Tempo primo: Vivace

Reger's quintet for clarinet, two violins, viola and cello, is a calm and serene piece, reminiscent of Brahms. Unusually the clarinet is not treated as the most important instrument here – the musical material is shared equally between each performer.

GREAT PLAYERS – EARLY

JOSEPH BEER
1744–1812

Joseph Beer was the first important solo clarinettist. He was born in Bohemia (present-day Czechoslovakia) where he first learnt the trumpet and later the clarinet. He moved to Paris where he concentrated on improving his clarinet playing, and became friends with Carl Stamitz, a keen composer of clarinet music. Beer soon made a name for himself as a virtuoso clarinettist, travelling all over Europe. From 1782–92 he was clarinettist to Catherine the Great of Russia, and was later employed by Frederick the Great of Prussia.

ANTON STADLER
1753–1812

Anton Stadler was born in Austria where he and his brother Johann both studied the clarinet, frequently performing together. In 1773 they were employed by the Russian ambassador in Vienna, and having made a name for themselves as musicians of excellence, were invited to join the orchestra of the royal court in 1787 as its first regular clarinettists.

Stadler designed a new instrument which could play much lower notes than the normal clarinet, calling his new model the 'basset' clarinet. He also wrote several works for the clarinet.

SIMON HERMSTEDT
1778–1846

As a child, Simon Hermstedt learnt several instruments, but it was as a clarinettist that he excelled. In 1801 notice of his playing reached a local member of the nobility, the Duke of Sondershausen, who engaged him as a court musician. The duke, impressed with his new musician, commissioned a concerto from the composer Spohr to be performed by Hermstedt and the ducal orchestra. As a performer Hermstedt played throughout Germany, astounding audiences with his technical brilliance.

GREAT PLAYERS – EARLY

THOMAS LINDSAY WILLMAN 1784–1840

Thomas Lindsay Willman was born into a musical family. His father was a German bandsman who settled in England in the middle of the eighteenth century, and his sister married the celebrated flautist Charles Nicholson.

At the age of twenty-one Willman played in the Dublin Theatre orchestra, and in 1916 took a permanent appointment as bandmaster to the Coldstream Guards. The following year he accepted the position of first clarinet in the Philharmonic orchestra and held this appointment until his death. In 1838 he gave the first English performance of Mozart's clarinet concerto.

HEINRICH BAERMANN 1784–1847

Like his close contemporary Simon Hermstedt, Heinrich Baermann was educated at a school for children of the military. By the age of fourteen he was an oboist in the band of the Prussian Life Guards, but he renounced this to study the clarinet with the famous virtuoso, Joseph Beer.

Baermann toured far and wide, performing the works written for him by Weber, Mendelssohn and Meyerbeer. In 1819 he visited England where he played before the Prince Regent at Brighton, and gave a series of concerts in London, playing several of his own works.

HYACINTHE ELÉONORE KLOSÉ 1808–1880

Hyacinthe Eléonore Klosé was born in Corfu, moving to Paris as a young man and enlisting in a regimental band as a clarinettist. In 1831 he entered the Paris Conservatoire, and was taught by Frédérick Berr. He played in orchestras, and made a name for himself as a soloist. Later he succeeded his teacher at the Conservatoire, where he remained for thirty years.

Klosé spent many years adapting the fingering of the new Boehm flute to the clarinet, as well as composing and publishing music for the instrument and writing an important tutor that is still used today.

GREAT PLAYERS – MODERN

RICHARD MÜHLFELD
1856–1907

Both violin and clarinet were important instruments to Richard Mühlfeld. His first major employment was as a court violinist in his home town of Meiningen and six years later, when he was twenty-three, he became principal clarinettist in the orchestra of the Duke of Meiningen.

It was the conductor of the court orchestra who pointed out the impressive playing of Mühlfeld to Brahms, and possibly suggested the composer might like to write for clarinet. The results brought both composer and performer success and pleasure.

MANUEL GOMEZ
1859–1922

Manuel Gomez was born in Seville, Spain, where a visiting bandmaster gave him clarinet lessons. In 1882 he gained admission to the Paris Conservatoire. After completing his studies he was appointed first clarinet at the Paris Opéra. In 1890 Gomez moved to London where he met and became firm friends with the conductor Henry Wood. In 1903 Gomez and a group of friends planned a new London orchestra – the London Symphony Orchestra – which gave its first performance in 1904. Although he gave solo recitals throughout his life, Gomez was primarily a skilled orchestral player.

FREDERICK THURSTON
1901–1953

Frederick Thurston won an open scholarship to London's Royal College of Music. His professional life began with the Royal Philharmonic Orchestra and the Covent Garden Opera orchestra. Later he played with the BBC's own Symphony Orchestra, and returned to the Royal College of Music to teach.

Frederick Thurston inspired several British composers to write works for him, including Arnold Bax (clarinet sonata), and Arthur Bliss (clarinet quintet).

GREAT PLAYERS – MODERN

BENNY GOODMAN
1909–1986

The American Benny Goodman entered the world of clarinet playing through jazz. At the age of twelve he made his professional début and, still in his teens, joined a professional band as a soloist.

In 1934 Benny Goodman took a step in another direction, and made several classical recordings, including Mozart's clarinet quintet, a shift in career which turned out to be astonishingly successful. He commissioned pieces from Bartók, Copland and Hindemith, and recorded many of the greatest works in the clarinet repertoire.

JACK BRYMER
born 1915

The British clarinettist Jack Brymer was born in the north of England to a musical family and taught himself to play the clarinet. In 1947 he was appointed principal clarinettist of the Royal Philharmonic Orchestra, after which he held the same position with the BBC Symphony Orchestra, and later with the London Symphony Orchestra.

Jack Brymer has been a founder member of several wind ensembles. He taught at the Royal Academy of Music and at the Royal Military School of Music. He has made three recordings of Mozart's clarinet concerto.

GERVASE DE PEYER
born 1926

Gervase de Peyer was born in London, where he studied under the British clarinettist Frederick Thurston at the Royal College of Music. In 1950 he formed and played in the Melos Ensemble. He also directed the London Symphony Wind Ensemble. In 1955 he was appointed first clarinet with the London Symphony Orchestra, a position he held until 1971. As a soloist, he has given many important first performances of clarinet works by British composers, including Thea Musgrave's clarinet concerto. Gervase de Peyer also teaches at London's Royal Academy of Music.

CD Track Listings

Figures in […] identify the track numbers from the EMI recording. Track lengths are listed in minutes and seconds

EMI is one of the world's leading classical music companies with a rich heritage and reputation for producing great and often definitive recordings performed by the world's greatest artists. As a result of this long and accomplished recording history, EMI has an exceptional catalogue of classical recordings, exceptional in both quality and quantity. It is from this catalogue that EMI have selected the recordings detailed in the track listing below. Many of the recordings featured are available on CD and cassette from EMI.

Wolfgang Amadeus Mozart 1756–1791
Clarinet Quintet in A K581
[1] I. Allegro — 6.49
Gervase de Peyer (clarinet)
Members of the Melos Ensemble of London
Ⓟ1964/1989*

Ludwig van Beethoven 1770–1827
Clarinet Trio in B flat Op. 11
[2] I. Allegro con brio — 8.58
The Nash Ensemble of London
Ⓟ1990†

Bernhard Crusell 1775–1838
Clarinet Concerto No. 2 in F minor Op. 5
[3] III. Rondo: Allegretto — 6.07
Antony Pay (clarinet)
Orchestra of the Age of Enlightenment Ⓟ1993†

Louis Spohr 1784–1859
Octet in E Op. 32
[4] Adagio – Allegro — 6.37
Members of the Melos Ensemble of London
Ⓟ1958/1995* [MONO]

Carl Maria von Weber 1786–1826
Grand Duo Concertant Op. 48
[5] III. Rondo: Allegro — 5.49
Michael Collins (clarinet)
Kathryn Stott (piano) Ⓟ1992

Gioachino Rossini 1792–1868
[6] **Introduction, Theme and Variations for
      clarinet and orchestra** — 12.56
Gervase de Peyer (clarinet)
New Philharmonia Orchestra conducted by
Rafael Frühbeck de Burgos Ⓟ1969/1986*

Felix Mendelssohn 1809–1847
**Concert Piece in D minor
for clarinet, basset-horn and orchestra No. 2** Op. 114
[7] Presto – Andante – Allegretto grazioso — 8.26
Sabine Meyer (clarinet) Wolfgang Meyer (basset-horn)
Württemberg Chamber Orchestra Heilbronn
conducted by Jörg Faerber Ⓟ1985+

Robert Schumann 1810–1856
Phantasiestücke Op. 73
[8] III. Rasch und mit Feuer – Coda: Schneller — 4.08
Michael Collins (clarinet) Kathryn Stott (piano) Ⓟ1992

Johannes Brahms 1833–1897
Clarinet Quintet in B minor Op. 115
[9] III. Andantino – Presto non assai, ma con sentimento — 4.44
Gervase de Peyer (clarinet)
Members of the Melos Ensemble of London Ⓟ1965/1989*

Max Reger 1873–1916
Clarinet Quintet in A Op. 146
[10] II. Vivace – Un poco meno mosso –
      Tempo primo: Vivace — 5.33
Gervase de Peyer (clarinet)
Members of the Melos Ensemble of London Ⓟ1965/1995*

70.50
[DDD/*ADD]